A NOTE TO PARENTS

When your children are ready to "step into reading," giving them the right books—and lots of them—is as crucial as giving them the right food to eat. **Step into Reading Books** present exciting stories and information reinforced with lively, colorful illustrations that make learning to read fun, satisfying, and worthwhile. They are priced so that acquiring an entire library of them is affordable. And they are beginning readers with an important difference—they're written on four levels.

Step 1 Books, with their very large type and extremely simple vocabulary, have been created for the very youngest readers. **Step 2 Books** are both longer and slightly more difficult. **Step 3 Books,** written to mid-second-grade reading levels, are for the child who has acquired even greater reading skills. **Step 4 Books** offer exciting nonfiction for the increasingly proficient reader.

Children develop at different ages. **Step into Reading Books,** with their four levels of reading, are designed to help children become good—and interested—readers *faster*. The grade levels assigned to the four steps—preschool through grade 1 for Step 1, grades 1 through 3 for Step 2, grades 2 and 3 for Step 3, and grades 2 through 4 for Step 4—are intended only as guides. Some children move through all four steps very rapidly; others climb the steps over a period of several years. These books will help your child "step into reading" in style!

For Alexander —J.C.

For Abigail, Jennifer, and Amanda —M.H.

Library of Congress Cataloging-in-Publication Data:
Cole, Joanna. Bully trouble / by Joanna Cole : illustrated by Marylin Hafner.   p.   cm.—(Step into reading. A step 2 book) SUMMARY: Arlo and Robby, finding themselves the victims of a neighborhood bully, work out a red-hot scheme for discouraging him.   ISBN: 0-394-84949-3 (pbk.); 0-394-94949-8 (lib. bdg.)   [1. Bullies—Fiction] I. Hafner, Marylin, ill. II. Title. III. Series: Step into reading. Step 2 book.   PZ7.C67346Bu   1990   [E]—dc19   89-3757

Manufactured in the United States of America   14   15   16   17   18   19   20

STEP INTO READING is a trademark of Random House, Inc.

Step into Reading

Bully Trouble

By Joanna Cole
Illustrated by Marylin Hafner

A Step 2 Book

Random House 🏠 New York

Arlo and Robby were on

the Wolf Cubs baseball team.

They had new caps,

new shirts,

and new gloves.

When the Wolf Cubs won,

everyone went thumbs up!

That meant

"We are the greatest!"

Every day

Arlo and Robby met in front

of the red house on the corner.

Then they walked

to the ball field together.

6

One day

Arlo left his house early.

He took his ball and glove

and a bag of chips.

He got to the red house

before Robby.

Soon a big kid came by.

"I'm Eddie," said the kid.

"Hi," said Arlo.

"I bet you can't
jump over that puddle,"
said Eddie.
"You are too little."

Arlo got mad.

"I am not!" he said.

"Just watch me!"

Arlo ran and jumped.

Eddie put out his foot.

Arlo went flying.

SPLAT!

He fell in the puddle.

Eddie laughed and laughed.

"You tripped me!" said Arlo.

He was so mad

that tears came to his eyes.

"So long, crybaby!" said Eddie.

"And thanks for the chips!"

Just then Robby ran up.

"I saw what happened.

That Big Eddie is so mean," said Robby.

Arlo wiped the tears away.

He wiped off his new shirt.

Then Arlo and Robby

went to the ball field.

Playing ball was fun.

Arlo forgot about Big Eddie.

Arlo hit the ball.

He ran

to second base.

Then Robby hit the ball

and Arlo ran all the way home.

"Yay, Arlo!

Yay, Robby!"

yelled the team.

Everyone went thumbs up.

"We are the greatest!"

On the way home
Robby said,
"I wish I had a soda."
"Me too," said Arlo.
Robby and Arlo
looked in their pockets.
They each had a little money.
"We can get one soda
and share it,"
said Robby.

Arlo and Robby

went into the store.

They asked the lady

for one soda and two straws.

"You must be best friends,"

said the lady in the store.

"This is a Best-Friends' Special!"

Arlo and Robby went outside.

They put their baseball gloves

on the ground.

They started to drink the soda.

"Oh no," said Arlo.

"Look who is coming."

It was Big Eddie.

"That is a nice glove, kid,"

Eddie said to Robby.

Eddie picked up Robby's glove.

"Hey! Give that back!"

yelled Robby.

"Okay," said Big Eddie.

He threw the glove way up high.

It landed on the roof
of the store.
"Take your glove, kid,"
said Big Eddie.
He picked up the soda
and ran down the street.
"Thanks for the soda,"
he called back.

The lady from the store
helped Arlo and Robby
get the glove down.

Then Arlo and Robby went back
to Robby's house.

In Robby's kitchen
they got two sodas
and drank them down.
But they were still mad.
"I hate it when Big Eddie
picks on us," said Arlo.
"I wish we could stop him."
Robby looked at his empty soda can.
It gave him an idea.
"Maybe we <u>can</u> stop him.
Eddie likes to take our stuff.
Let's give him a big treat.
One Bully Special coming up!"

Robby got out a bowl.

He put in a little vinegar,

a little steak sauce,

and a <u>lot</u> of prune juice.

He mixed it all around.

It looked horrible.

Arlo and Robby poured it

into the empty soda can.

Arlo said, "This is great!"

"Wait, there is more,"

Robby told him.

Robby went to the refrigerator.

He got out a jar.

"What is that?" asked Arlo.

"Chili sauce," said Robby.

"Try it.

But just take a little bit."

Arlo took a tiny, tiny bit.

YIKES!

It made his whole mouth burn!

Arlo and Robby made
one hot chili sandwich.

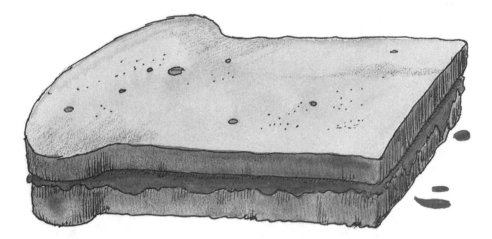

They made one jam sandwich.

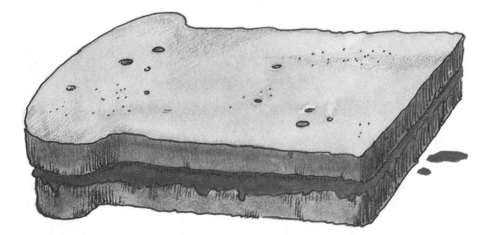

Both sandwiches looked the same.

They put them in Robby's lunchbox.

"Watch out, Big Eddie!" said Arlo.

"Here we come!"

Arlo and Robby went to the park.

There was Eddie!

He was watching some big kids

play basketball.

Arlo took the jam sandwich

out of the lunchbox.

He started to eat it.

"Yum!" said Arlo in a loud voice.

"I just love this sandwich."

Eddie came over.

Arlo took out

the hot chili sandwich.

Eddie grabbed it.

"This looks good,"

he said.

"Too bad <u>you</u> won't get to eat it."

He smiled

and licked his lips.

Then he took a big bite.

His face turned red.

Tears rolled down his cheeks.

"YOW-EEEE!" he yelled.

"That stuff is HOT!"

Robby held up the soda can.

Eddie grabbed it

and took a big gulp.

"YUCK!"

Eddie held his throat.

"POO-EEE!"

Eddie ran for the water fountain.

Arlo and Robby laughed.

The big kids laughed too.

"Eddie will not bother you anymore,"
they said.

"He only picks on kids
who let him get away with it."

44

Arlo and Robby started home.

"I wish I had a soda,"

said Arlo.

"Me too," said Robby.

Arlo and Robby went to the store.

"One Best-Friends' Special, please,"

they said to the lady.

"Coming up!"

said the lady.

She gave them one soda.

She put two straws in it.

Arlo and Robby drank their soda together.

Then they went thumbs up!

"We are the greatest!"